The Great Train Robbery

THE GREAT TRAIN ROBBERY

The 1896 Western Melodrama

A Play in Four Acts

by Scott Marble

Theatre Arts Press

9 8 7 6 5 4 3 2 1

THE GREAT TRAIN ROBBERY

The 1896 Western Melodrama

A Play in Four Acts

by Scott Marble

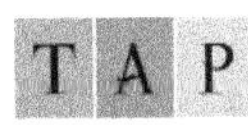

Theatre Arts Press

9 8 7 6 5 4 3 2 1

CHARACTERS

Tom Gordon, cashier of the Wells-Fargo Express Company

Sam Carter, chief clerk of Wells-Fargo Express Company

Dan Hollis, clerk, allis Jack Baker

Bronco Joe, Deputy U.S. Marshal, owner of the Never Shut Saloon

William Bennett, superintendent of the Wells-Fargo Express

Sergeant Flynn of 6th Cavalry

Joshua Glue, sooner wrestle than eat

Solitaire, a weary son of Mars, champion liar of the world

Peanuckle Schilitz, trying to express a telephone

Texas Jake

Tip Porter

John Sherley, telegraph operator and station agent

Jim Judson, barkeep

Rattlesnake Pete, a terror

Expressman

Express messenger

Louise Gordon

Alice Bennett

Maggie Murphy

Rose Wilson

Fanny Knight

Laura Dorn

Mary Lee

Synopsis of Scenes

Act One
Wells-Fargo Express Office, Kansas City

Act Two
"The Never Shut" Saloon, Red Rock, one month later

Act Three
Wichita Mountains

Act Four
Scene 1
Red River Canyon, morning

Scene 2
Dug out with roof made of logs and straw

Scene 3
The Broken Boulder Trail

Scene 4
The dug out, Red River Canon

Act One

Wells-Fargo Express Office, Kansas City.

Barrels, boxes, packages on floor, packages on counter, scales, maps hanging on flats.

Enter Tip with a number of packages.

TIP. I'm tired of this ye work. Why can't people keep der trunk at home. Nobody ever sends me anything. *(Falls over box.)* I knew it! I'll get killed in this place yet.

(Enter Flynn with small box. Uniform of U.S. soldier.)

FLYNN. Hallo. Can a man send a box to Red Rock, Red River Township, Dead Man County, Winship P.O. Indian Territory, United States of America?

TIP. I don't know sah. You will have to wait until the puzzle man comes in.

FLYNN. What the devil is the puzzle man?

TIP. Why der man what tells yer where to send your package when yer don't know yourself.

FLYNN. I'll break your jaw.

TIP *(close to Flynn)*. Whose jaw?

FLYNN. Your jaw.

TIP. What for?

FLYNN. Your saying I don't know where I'll send this box.

TIP. The puzzle man don't know it.

FLYNN. Did I say he did?

TIP. But the man don't know it.

FLYNN. What man?

TIP. The puzzle man.

FLYNN. I don't care a damn if he never knows it. I am here to ship a box over the express.

TIP. Did I say yar wasn't?

FLYNN. What the devil do you do here, anyway?

TIP *(going to back of counter)*. That's my business. I'm only here loosely.

FLYNN. Loosely?

TIP. Yes, I anticipate my 'piantment as car porter, and am only hanging 'round waiting fo' it. Where's yer box?

(He places on scales.)

FLYNN. Do yer weight everything?

TIP. You bet we do — want to pay da charges?

FLYNN. Aw course I do. What are they?

TIP *(looks over book)*. Eleven — dollars and forty cents.

FLYNN. What?

TIP. Cash.

FLYNN. You'd better send it collect.

TIP. Can't do it, sah. Dir company ain't toting anything for nothing.

FLYNN. Come out of that! Come here where I can get at you. I'll show you how a Sergeant of the 26th can dress you up. You won't come? Then I'll go after yer.

TIP *(leaning over counter, rises, holding large revolver)*. You can't dress anything in here. You take that box and skip out. I'm a bud from Pine Street and I hold my record. Ship!

FLYNN. No sir! An Irishman never turns his back to the enemy; shot and be damned! And if ye do shoot, I'll have the satisfaction of seeing ye hung.

(Enter Carter.)

CARTER. Here! What's the matter? Tip, put up that gun. Now sir, who are you?

FLYNN. Sergeant Flynn of the 26th on a furlough. I came in here like a decent man to send this box when he charged me eleven dollars and forty cents.

TIP. Can't blame me, sir. All de clerks like to be dead sure dat de charges cover every thing.

CARTER. Go back to your work! *(Tip retires.)* I will take your package sir. *(Weights it.)* $1.40, sir.

FLYNN. Sure, and that's more decent.

CARTER. You are stationed in the Red River Country?

FLYNN. Yes, but I have me furlough I'm on to see Miss Murphy.

CARTER. The servant at Mr. Bennett's?

FLYNN. That's the same.

CARTER. Have you been calling at the house?

FLYNN. For over a week now. Mr. Bennett is a fine gentleman, and his daughter is the finest looker I ever met. And if Mr. Gordon don't marry her he's a fool.

CARTER. Do you mean to say that Mr. Gordon calls at the house?

FLYNN. Calls, is it? Faith and I found him there every evening, and one night last week Miss Alice invited us all to the theatre. Sure, and it is in love with each other they are.

CARTER. You are mistaken, sir. Well, here is your receipt. When do you return to the Fort?

FLYNN. Well, the Lord be willing and the cars do be running, late this night. Good luck to ya. *(Aside.)* He didn't like the news. I do believe he loves Miss Bennett a bit himself. *(To the door.)* If ever I find that Tip I'll pulverize him.

(He exits.)

CARTER. I cannot imagine that Alice would encourage Gordon.

(Enter Dan Hollis.)

HOLLIS. Ah, good morning, Carter. Didn't see you at the theatre last evening. Gordon and Miss Bennett occupied a box. Has Tom cut you out?

CARTER. Oh no.

HOLLIS. Your faith in a woman is refreshing. You were away on the road two months and the moment your back is turned, she falls in love with Gordon. Now they are engaged. You see he is a more ardent lover than you are.

CARTER. Impossible. You can't arouse my jealousy, Hollis.

HOLLIS. I have no desire to arouse your jealousy. Simply to guide a blind man. Miss Bennett is in love with Tom Gordon.

CARTER. You judge from appearances.

HOLLIS. Certainly when a young lady of wealthy parents has her breakfast at seven o'clock in the morning in order to accompany her father's cashier to the office, I am impressed that she loves him.

CARTER. I do not believe it.

HOLLIS. If I should convince you of its truth, what then?

CARTER. If this man Gordon has taken advantage of my absence to undermine me in the estimation of Alice Bennett I will not rest until I get even with the treacherous man.

HOLLIS. If he falls in love with the lady and gains possession of her heart, what can you do? The law forbids dueling. To assault him would lead to unpleasant notoriety.

CARTER. I would find a way to revenge myself.

HOLLIS. There is only one way, Carter. Bankrupt Bennett. Then Alice will be poor instead of marrying into luxury. Gordon would be complied to earn a living. Alice Bennett would regret ever having married him and possibly leave him. What a revenge.

CARTER. How would you accomplish this?

HOLLIS. I will tell you after you have been convinced that Miss Bennett intends to marry Tom Gordon.

CARTER. Oh no Hollis. I never cross a bridge until I come to it.

HOLLIS. Well in this instance you will have no bridge to cross.

(He retires up right. Enter Joshua Glue.)

JOSHUA. Be this the shipping office of The Overland Express?

CARTER. Yes sir.

JOSHUA. Want to buy any wood?

CARTER. No sir.

JOSHUA. If I put a parcel in here, when will it get to where I want to send it?

CARTER. To what point?

JOSHUA. Taint on point. Beef Cut Creek, Calamity County, Idaho.

CARTER. Where is your package?

JOSHUA. What package?

CARTER. The one you wish to express.

JOSHUA. Oh, I ain't going to send it till Christmas. Jest wanted to know. I came here to see about this card. *(Hands postal card.)* Your folks sent it.

CARTER. Your name is Joshua Glue?

JOSHUA. That's it. Born Glue. Named Joshua.

CARTER. From what place do you expect a package?

JOSHUA. Can't tell till I see it.

CARTER. You must have someone to identify you.

JOSHUA. Identify me? Do you suspect me? Why you lantern jawed dude, I want you to know I'm no green money fool. Want the police to identify me, eh?

CARTER. I simply want to know that you are Joshua Glue.

JOSHUA. Didn't I jest tell yer?

CARTER. That won't do. You must bring some one here whom we know that can assert you are the real Joshua Glue.

JOSHUA. Some one you know, eh? Do you think I've nothing else to do but run around pool rooms, poker games, Dude Clubs looking up your folks? I want that parcel or by Jimmy Christopher there's going to be a meeting right here. *(Pounds on counter.)*

CARTER. You won't get it until you are identified. Rule of the company, sir.

JOSHUA. Want to keep if for yourself, eh? Young man, up in my country I'm known as the Prime Minster on wrestling, and the Duke of Gooseberry on rough and tumbling, so I'll just identify myself.

(He springs over counter and is seized by Carter. They struggle through gate to counter, to centre, when Joshua trips Carter and he falls.)

JOSHUA. Get up, yer darn dodo and I'll take another fall out of yer. I'll satisfy yer I'm Joshua Glue.

CARTER. You infernal fool.

(He rushes at Glue who dodges the blow, seizes him, trips him and Carter goes down.)

JOSHUA. Come again, plenty more left.

(Enter Tip.)

TIP *(runs to centre)*. What's the matter here?

CARTER *(springing up)*. Hold that man until I send for an officer.

JOSHUA. No you don't. *(Seizes Carter as he is about to exit left when Tip seizes Joshua by collar. Joshua turns, trips up Tip who falls. Then Joshua throws arms around Carter, trips him, he falls. Joshua kneels between them hand on throat of each.)* Lost yer wind, eh? Satisfied yet, neighbor?

(Enter Bennett.)

BENNETT. Why, what is this?

JOSHUA. Little sport, want to join in? I was satisfying this dude that I am Joshua Glue.

(Tip jumps up and exits.)

CARTER. This man assaulted me because I demanded an identification.

JOSHUA. I reckon yer know me now. Ain't mad are yer? I'll go yer another.

BENNETT. This is rather a serious proceeding, sir.

JOSHUA. I should say it was — keeping a man's parcel.

BENNETT. What is the package, Mr. Carter? Money?

CARTER. No sir. I will get it. *(Back to counter.)*

BENNETT. Did you expect a package by express?

JOSHUA. No, hadn't laid out to get any.

CARTER *(hands small package)*. Mr. Bennett.

(Bennett goes back of counter, stands with back to audience, then turns.)

BENNETT. Do you remember, Mr. Glue, of ever writing to anyone for medicine?

JOSHUA. Cash, all hemlock, yes. I writ a doctor for hog medicine and sent him a dollar, and that's the last I heard of it.

BENNETT. Well, here it is. A little more patience, Mr. Carter, and I think you would have avoided trouble. Sign the book, Mr. Glue.

JOSHUA *(signs book)*. The trouble, Colonel, with that chap is he wanted to keep this hog medicine for himself. It's a mighty good thing you came in just as you did. Darn if it ain't! Good day, sir.

(He exits.)

BENNETT. Mr. Carter you must learn to curb your temper and use discretion. When Gordon arrives ask him to see me in the office.

(He exits. Enter Hollis carrying about fourteen feet of electric wire, a small phone receiver and speaking tube.)

HOLLIS. Well, Carter, I am going to make a test.

CARTER. In what way?

HOLLIS. Tap the phone. I place the receiver in my hat, hang it up on the rack near Bennett's desk, and the entire conversation can be heard through the tube. You will hear Gordon ask Bennett for Alice and then Bennett accepts him.

CARTER. He would not dare to ask for her hand.

HOLLIS. He is going to ask today for he told me so last night. But we will test it. Lock the door. *(Carter locks door and stands holding them while Hollis fastens wires to top of phone.)* Carry the wire under the counter and at that end — *(points right)* — close to the floor you will find a hole. Pass the wire through — I have it. *(Covers wire with mats, leading wire through door.)* Now I will make a connection with the receiver and place it in the hat.

CARTER *(to door left)*. Bennett will detect you.

HOLLIS. No. I simply hang up my hat. He cannot see through the glass partition, yet every word can be heard as the hat will hang a few inches higher than the partition. Unlock the door. And don't let anyone use the phone.

(He exits.)

CARTER. Can it be possible that Alice in accepting my intentions, never considered them seriously? No, I cannot believe it.

HOLLIS *(entering)*. All right. Now in the event of your being convinced, will you be guided by me?

CARTER. Yes.

HOLLIS. To any extent?

CARTER. To any extent for revenge.

HOLLIS. Good. I see you have spirit.

(He retires up stage. Enter Gordon and Alice.)

GORDON. Good morning, Mr. Carter. Glad to see you back at your old post.

CARTER. Mr. Gordon, Mr. Bennett desires to see you at once.

GORDON. I won't be but a moment, Alice.

(He exits.)

ALICE. Did you enjoy your trip, Mr. Carter?

CARTER. It was a relaxation from office work. Yet I found myself impatient to return after the first day.

ALICE. I love to travel, and I fancied you would have a delightful trip.

CARTER. Would you find pleasure in leaving your heart behind you? Alice, I loved you, and believing that you returned my affection, I gave no expression to it, save by action. It seems to me that you accepted my attentions by many little acts of consideration.

ALICE. Mr. Carter, never for a moment did it occur to me that you loved me. I would have been frank with you and discouraged it. You were an occasional visitor at my father's house, the same as many others whose kind invitation I accepted, not because I desired them particularly but to avoid giving offence.

CARTER. Alice, if ever woman was kind and affectionate you were with me, and so uniform was that treatment that I believed you love me. Alice, can you not realize what it all means to me?

ALICE. I am very sorry, Mr. Carter.

CARTER. Is it true that you are engaged to Mr. Gordon?

ALICE. Yes, Mr. Carter, we are engaged.

CARTER. Had I not introduced this man to you, you might have loved me. You did love me with a girlish affection, but this Gordon impressed you and you simply forgot me.

ALICE. You are very unjust.

CARTER. Unjust! Do you know what you have done? You have killed my faith in your sex. You have deaden my conscience and made me desperate, and this deception will find a way to punish the man who so outraged my confidence.

ALICE. What do you mean? Mr. Gordon has always been your friend.

CARTER. Friend? He knew that I loved you. I confessed it to him and like a fool believing in your love told him that you loved me. We had sat for hours speaking of you and I pictured a future. God! It was a delirium of love, a madness! He listened and encouraged me. He asked for an introduction. I was glad to do so, since I was sure of you, but the moment I left the city he used every art to win you, and he has succeeded.

ALICE. You can please whatever construction upon my conduct your jealous nature may imagine, since my avowal that you are wrong does not convince you. Had I never met Mr. Gordon, my relations with you would not have gone beyond friendship.

CARTER *(seizing her wrist)*. Do you fancy he can make you happy? He will ruin your life! He will drag you down to poverty, since he married you only for your father's money.

GORDON *(entering)*. Alice your father desires to see you. Why, your face is flushed, what is the matter? Has anything been said to offend you?

ALICE. No, no, it is nothing! How strangely you speak, Tom.

GORDON. What could have been said?

CARTER. There has been nothing discussed, sir, that I would not repeat to you, and with decidedly more strength or will and purpose.

GORDON. An opportunity will present itself for I believe that you have insulted Miss Bennett.

ALICE. Tom, never mind! It is nothing!

CARTER. Yes, I did insult her, if you like, and she deserves to be insulted by the man she has wronged.

GORDON. You —

ALICE. For my sake don't quarrel, Tom, please!

(She pushes him off.)

HOLLIS *(entering)*. Are you convinced? Listen at the phone, quick! *(Carter tube to ear.)* Can you hear?

CARTER. Gordon is going to take charge of a shipment of gold, fifty thousand dollars, twenty thousand of which belongs to Bennett. Bennett has just told Gordon he can marry Alice in San Francisco. *(Drops tube.)* No use. I can't endure the torture. *(Hollis jumps to tube.)* Alice has passed out of my life forever. *(At desk behind window, head on hands.)*

HOLLIS. The money is to go out tonight. Are you listening? Part for Tucson and part for Yuma to be invested in Bennett's mine. It will go over the Rock Island Road by the way of Fort Worth. Good! I know the country well, on this side of Red River. What's this? He is telling Bennett that you insulted Alice. Will have you discharged. Come man, arouse yourself! We will stop part of that gold at Red Rock and escape into the Wichita Mountain.

CARTER *(starting up)*. What do you mean?

HOLLIS. If Gordon fails to carry the gold through you may yet marry Alice. *(Replacing wires on phone, removing others.)* If we lose the game, we can charge Gordon with having tipped off the information and he will go down with us. That is your revenge!

CARTER. And if we succeed?

HOLLIS. You are twenty thousand ahead and that is pretty good salve for a heart ache. Will you do it?

CARTER. Yes, and with a desperation born of madness.

HOLLIS. Now to remove my hat.

(He exits. Enter Peanuckle Schlitz.)

PEANUCKLE *(with small box)*. Vass dere some places already what I send over a box mit a phone.

CARTER. No, our phone is out of order.

PEANUCKLE. Den I don't send a box mit a phone.

CARTER. Who sent you in here to ask such a question?

PEANUCKLE. Your sign was on de outside, so I came in once.

CARTER. Well, you can't send a box by phone. You should know better. A phone is to speak through.

PEANUCKLE. Yes, I dink so myself. Den I can't send a box mit a phone, up right side mis glass.

CARTER. You leather headed Dutchman, do you know yourself what you want?

PEANUCKLE. I don't speak me very fine English yet. So I don't make yourself understood by me. I was going by Red River, and I want to send a box wit a phone.

CARTER. Go down the street two blocks.

PEANUCKLE. Den I come back, eh?

CARTER. No, no. Get out!

HOLLIS *(entering with hat)*. Well, Gordon is riding a high horse. He says the office staff should be changed.

PEANUCKLE. Den I send me my box, ain't it?

CARTER. Hollis get rid of this Dutchman. Some fool sent him here as a joke.

HOLLIS. What is it, sir?

PEANUCKLE. I send me out a phone mit a box.

HOLLIS. Where are you going?

PEANUCKLE. Place what you call Rush Springs. My friend has a beer saloon and I make myself barkeep, right away.

HOLLIS. Red River country, eh?

PEANUCKLE. I want to send my box mit a phone out.

HOLLIS. What have you in the box?

PEANUCKLE. A phone.

HOLLIS. Oh! And you want to send it to King Fisher. That is on the main line. What is your name?

PEANUCKLE. Peanuckle Schlitz.

HOLLIS. Go over there and weigh yourself. *(Peanuckle goes to scales. To Carter.)* This fellow is just stupid enough to answer my purpose. To meet such a deal as this I had ordered several small boxes, in imitation of the gold shipment boxes. They are packed with lead and ready.

CARTER. What do you intend?

HOLLIS. Send this Dutchman with an order to have the boxes delivered here. Then when the gold boxes arrive, change the boxes. *(Writes.)* Here Peanuckle take this note. Any one will direct you. You needn't come back. Your phone is all right.

PEANUCKLE. Den I go mis dis.

(He exits.)

CARTER. Have you confidence in a change of boxes?

HOLLIS. I have never known it to fail. No one will detect the difference until they are opened. I will have time to imitate the marks and address. Don't lose your nerve. We will succeed.

(He retires back. Enter Gordon. Phone rings.)

GORDON. Hello, yes, Gordon, cashier. You won't send the gold today. Yes, I understand, all right, goodbye. *(Rings off.)* I was to happy in the contemplation of having Alice with me, there is always something to come up and mar our happiness.

(Enter Alice.)

ALICE. I'm going home to pack. What a lovely trip we will have.

GORDON. Yes, the bank just telephoned me that there would be a delay.

(Enter Bennett.)

ALICE. I am so disappointed, papa.

BENNETT. About what, my child?

ALICE. Why our trip, of course. I wouldn't see much of Tom on our way out but coming back we could be together. Now it is all upset by the mean old bank.

BENNETT. No. We go just the same only later in the week and Gordon shall be guardian of both. *(Arms about her.)*

ALICE. Thank you, papa, I will drive home at once.

(Enter Maggie Murphy with a very small trunk.)

MAGGIE *(stumbles in)*. The devil's in this same box for I've done nothing but fall over it and — *(Looks up, sees Alice.)* Why Miss Alice.

ALICE. Maggie, what brings you here?

MAGGIE. I'm going out with the Sergeant to Red Rock. He says the ground out there is full of gold and I can help myself.

ALICE. Are you really going to marry?

MAGGIE. Not until the Sergeant leaves the sojer business. He has four months to serve, then we will open a gold mine or a saloon, it's all the same.

GORDON. Then you are going to leave us?

MAGGIE. Yes sir, the wife must follow the husband. But I'll be going as far as Red Rock wid yez, and here's me bit of a trunk.

ALICE. Maggie, we are not going tonight, but later in the week.

MAGGIE. Sure I can wait if you will keep the trunk for me.

BENNETT. You may leave it. Mr. Carter will you kindly attend to it?

(Carter takes trunk back.)

ALICE. I will go, papa.

(Over, kissing him. Up to Gordon. Bennett turns looks at watch. Maggie looking out of door. Alice kisses Gordon and runs off followed by Maggie.)

BENNETT. I will stop at the bank and ascertain the cause of the delay. No one is aware of this gold shipment except yourself and Alice, the bank president, his cashier and myself.

GORGON. There is no way by which any one except ourselves can learn of the shipment and you may feel quite safe on that score.

PEANUCKLE *(entering)*. Vas does boxes what come by me youst not.

CARTER *(from back)*. Stop your noise. What is it?

PEANUCKLE. Some boxes what I get me. Here he was.

(Enter Expressman carrying three small boxes. Stripe of sheet torn bound at each end, places them on stage near counter and exits.)

HOLLIS *(with marking pot, down from back)*. I am all ready. Say Duchy, you go out and help the driver.

PEANUCKLE. Do I get a beer?

HOLLIS. Yes. Go, go!

(Peanuckle exits. Hollis begins marking boxes.)

CARTER. Won't they detect the difference in the marking?

HOLLIS. No. When the gold comes, we'll hustle it away leaving these boxes. *(Enter Expressman and Peanuckle with three boxes each and exit.)* Stand by the door. *(Marks boxes.)* Now we are all right.

CARTER *(to desk)*. I suppose the next thing will be my discharge. Well, I am ready for anything now.

HOLLIS. I hope so. Then you will be free to hide the gold.

(Bennett and Gordon enter.)

BENNETT *(looking at boxes)*. Tucson — Yuma. *(Aside to Gordon.)* Can this be the gold shipment?

GORDON. I hardly think so. They would not mark it lead.

(Enter Peanuckle.)

GORDON. Did these come in our wagon?

CARTER. No sir. By private express.

GORDON *(aside to Bennett)*. They would not risk shipment in this way.

BENNETT. It is certainly strange.

CARTER. Mr. Hollis, here is a shipment of lead to Yuma and Tucson.

BENNETT. Wait a moment. Open one of those boxes.

CARTER. They are marked lead.

BENNETT. Whoever sent them used boxes usually employed for gold. Open that box!

CARTER *(opens box)*. Lead sir.

BENNETT. Open another.

CARTER *(opens box)*. Lead.

BENNETT. Singular! Lead is not shipped in this way and never to my knowledge from this office. It appears to me that an attempt is being made to substitute these boxes for those of the gold. I will investigate this thoroughly.

PEANUCKLE. I know noddings. I was out by me for —

CARTER. This man came in about an hour ago and asked the rates to Montana. He speaks poor English.

PEANUCKLE. You was a liar. I talk out yeust as plain so you can't.

BENNETT. This is all very suspicious.

GORDON. That man can explain, he brought the goods.

CARTER. Mr. Bennett, the man knows nothing. Still it's no secret about this gold shipment.

BENNETT. What is this?

CARTER. $30,000 was to be sent West. $20,000 of which belonged to you and was to be invested in the Bennett mine. Mr. Gordon was to have had charge of it accompanied by your daughter. They were to have left tonight and been married in San Francisco.

BENNETT. Answer me sir. Did my daughter speak of this matter?

CARTER. No, sir.

(Enter Tip from back and remains behind desk.)

BENNETT. What you have said is absolutely secret and was official business of this company. From whom did you receive this information?

CARTER. I would rather not say sir.

BENNETT. Speak or I will force it from you in a court of justice. Who betrayed the confidence of this company?

CARTER *(pointing)*. That man! Tom Gordon.

HOLLIS. And I am witness!

GORDON. Liar!

(He starts at Carter when Bennett holds him back. Carter smiles at Gordon. Arms folded. Gordon in attitude of reaching over Bennett's arm. Hollis at back as if about to join Carter in case Gordon should reach him. Tip leaning over counter. Peanuckle half out of door.)

Quick Curtain

End of Act One

Act Two

"The Never Shut" Saloon, Red Rock. One month later.

An old clap board house or dilapidated kitchen. Doors right and left. Wood or landscape drop or flats back of windows. Room for action. Table and chairs, common.

Discovered Bronco Joe behind bar cleaning glasses. Attire black pants, flannel shirt, belt, vest open. No coat. Pistol in hip pocket. Carter and Hollis, both wearing short beards, flannel shirts, short coats, belts, no vest, felt hat. Characters to dress as above (not the Western dress of 20 years ago.) Each character carries a pistol in hip pocket, not in belt.

HOLLIS. What ails you man? You set as if you regretted your revenge.

CARTER. No. But after all the gold may not come and we have simply thrown away position and reputation.

HOLLIS. Nonsense! You would have been discharged had you failed to resign. I told you, Carter, we started out to get rich quick, and I am going to do it. The gold will be on No. 10, reaching here tomorrow night.

CARTER. Are you sure?

HOLLIS. My man is no fool. He expects his bit of it and is just as anxious as we are. Have you seen that Irish Sergeant?

CARTER. Yes, but he failed to recognize me. He had heard no news from Kansas City except that Gordon had left the city.

HOLLIS. The old man will never permit Gordon to marry his daughter. Cheer up oh boy, you may win Alice yet.

BRONCO JOE. Do either of you gents know a street in New York by the name of Avenue A?

HOLLIS. I do, why?

BRONCO JOE. Nice neighborhood?

HOLLIS. Yes. Why do you ask?

BRONCO JOE *(to centre)*. Last fall I was prospecting up on the Sweetwater when I fell in love with another man's horse. Got that? The horse took a fancy to me and we eloped. I was awful fond of horse. Well, the sheriff got jealous and rounded me up. Got that?

CARTER. Caught, eh?

BRONCO JOE. Yes sir, and I was about to dance on air when Vchell, the U. S. Marshall came along and broke up the party, got that? I said I was drunk when I took the horse, apologized to the owner, had drinks all round —

HOLLIS. Horse returned of course.

BRONCO JOE. You can bet on that or I wouldn't be here today, an honest saloon keeper, got that? Last spring, the Marshall was held up by road agents who had a grudge agin him. They were fighting pretty lively, when I came along and popped over two of them and saved the Marshall.

CARTER. One good turn deserves another.

BRONCO JOE. He was badly hurt and a week after he died before telling me about his child in New York and asking me to look after him. Frances was the name, the address, Avenue A.

HOLLIS. Boy or girl?

BRONCO JOE. Didn't say. It was not a legitimate kid so he couldn't put the name in the will on account of his family, got that? So, he give me the cash to save. Well, I bought this place for the kid and am waiting for it to turn up.

CARTER. Did you ever find any trace of the child?

BRONCO JOE. Yes, got letter asking for full particulars, which I sent and have heard nothing since.

HOLLIS. How old is the child?

BRONCO JOE. Fifteen or sixteen.

CARTER. The chances are you will never hear anything about the claim unless some smart-aleck gets up a scheme to plant a boy and work him off on you as the heir.

HOLLIS. Asking for full particulars would indicate that. You must be careful Joe.

BRONCO JOE. They won't fool me. The Marshall gave me the brand — I mean the marks to identify.

(Enter Solitaire, a tramp solider. Army pants light blue, patched bars and three army cloth of different shades of blue. Single breasted coat. Patched on one arm (left). Right arm sleeve entire made from a piece of army blanket, dark or light in shade. Coat on one side patched. Four different badges on breast of coat. Army of cap of '61. One shoe built up to make a limp. Carries stick, short beard, face dirty, hair long.)

SOLITAIRE. Gents, I salute you. Lovely weather. This sal-lute-ray climate reminds me of the days with Hooker in the wilderness. I saved the life of General Catchpetter. *(Touches badge.)*

CARTER. Are you still in the army, Mr. — ?

SOLITAIRE. My name is Bunsen, but I'm known as Solitaire because twenty-five rebel sharp shooters tried to kill me. Did you notice my medals? No, I left the army about four years ago and went East but I couldn't stand it. I love the exciting Western life so came back among the boys. Why, sir, I can't breathe the air without a soldier in it somewhere.

HOLLIS. Have a drink, Solitaire?

SOLITAIRE. A little bit early for me, but I won't shoot a shingle off the roof. Make it better root nectar, Joe. Don't think I came in for this drink, gents. Before I left the army, I presented the government with a plan how to distribute Indians on the reservations to vaccinate 'em without pain. Notice this? *(Touches badge #2.)*

BRONCO JOE. Here's your drinks, gents.

(All take glasses.)

SOLITAIRE. Looking at you gents, while we watch the shallows. Say, Joe, there's a box for you at the depot so I asked Jim Curley to fetch it over.

BRONCO JOE. Box for me?

SOLITAIRE. Your name in plain letters. *(Drinks, gasps, coughs almost gags.)* By god that's good whiskey.

(Enter props and carpenter carrying a box two feet wide. Same in length. Five and a half high. Two holes on side. Stand box upright.)

BRONCO JOE. It's for me sure enough. *(To carpenter and props at bar.)* Have a drink boys?

SOLITAIRE *(up to bar for drink)*. I will never forget a box I opened once before Vicksburg. I was standing alongside of Sherman watching and dodging shells, when I happened to look behind a bush and there was a box, just as if it had dropped out of a wagon. It looked like a Christmas box filled with good things to eat.

HOLLIS. What was in it?

SOLITAIRE. Quinine pills.

BRONCO JOE *(from bar with hammer)*. Well, this is no Christmas box. If it's anything, it's hog meat. *(Opens box, pull off front.)*

(Louise Gordon disguised as boy, springs out.)

LOUISE. Well, here I am. Are you Bronco Joe?

BRONCO JOE. Great Ceaser!

CARTER *(starting up)*. That voice is familiar.

LOUISE. Did I scare you fellows? It was the only way I could get here. Come by slow freight. I'm Frank Vashell?

HOLLIS *(to Carter)*. I have heard that voice before, but I can't place it.

(Carpenter and Props exit. Solitaire takes another drink, watching Bronco Joe.)

BRONCO JOE *(aside to Louise)*. Have you any mark on yer, anywhere?

LOUISE. Yes, my arm has a sour from a burn.

CARTER. Joe, you had better make sure you have the right hog meat.

BRONCO JOE. Don't you interfere. Whether he is what he says or not, that cuts no ice with me. I like his face and he took a hard trip to reach me and I'm damned if I turn him loose in these hills to starve.

LOUISE. I like you. You're up and up. *(Turns to Hollis.)* You blokes are no good and you won't find no hog meat, I can tell you. Say Joe, on the level, I'm nearly starved.

BRONCO JOE. Here, here. *(Opens door.)* Go right in and help yourself. *(Exit Louise.)* I like that chap. Sol, you can have the box for a coffin.

SOLITAIRE. I'll take it. I remember once when I stood talking to Sheridan at the fight before —

BRONCO JOE. Get along out of here and stop your lying.

SOLITAIRE. Joe, you have hurt my feelings.

BRONCO JOE. Take a drink.

(Solitaire takes drink, picks up box and drags if off. Bronco Joe exits.)

CARTER *(aside to Hollis)*. When the boy goes out, follow him. We must not be recognized by any one from Kansas City.

HOLLIS. The boy came from New York. It is only a coincidence. Many people have voices alike. Don't borrow trouble. *(Enter Gordon and Judson.)* Here at last, eh? We have waited here all morning. Well, hot is it?

(Gordon stands at back near bar watching Carter.)

JUDSON. Crazy Dog will be here tonight.

HOLLIS. He understands what is wanted?

JUDSON. Of course. He will have his men near the gully and hold up the engineer.

CARTER. Real Indians?

JUDSON. No. That's only to make the passengers believe they were stopped by injuns. An injun will scare 'em more. Besides the sheriff will look for them, so we are safe.

CARTER. Who came in with you?

JUDSON. Doc Holliday, the fare dealer. Say Doc, give a handshake to Bill and Jack Baker.

(He retires behind bar. Apron on.)

GORDON *(does not offer to shake hands.)* Glad to know you. What's your coffin varnish, gents?

HOLLIS. Thank you we have got a drink. Are you dealing cards here, Mr. Holliday?

GORDON. No sir. I left El Paso a month ago where I had been dealing. No. I'm open for anything that has money in it.

(Enter Bronco Joe and Louise.)

BRONCO JOE. Never mind, Frank. Just take out the glasses and give them a gargle at the pump.

HOLLIS. What do you think of the idea?

GORDON. Well, I'll think it over.

(Exit Louise)

CARTER. Excuse me for a moment.

JUDSON. Hello, who's the kid?

BRONCO JOE. He's my boy, got that? And I want him respected. Got that? Then you hold on to it and don't forget. Fill up that whiskey bottle with water. I'm going to order some bear meat for the kid.

(He exits.)

GORDON. In case I take a hand in the deal, what do I get?

HOLLIS. We share alike.

(Scream outside by Louise. She rushes on followed by Carter. Bronco Joe enters seizes Carter and turns him to right and stands in front of Louise. Carter draws pistol. Gordon seizes his wrist.)

GORDON. None of that.

BRONCO JOE *(pistol in hand).* There's the door for you two and don't you come in here again. You have a spite agin the boy for some reason and if either of you ever attempt to harm him I'll kill yer on sight. Got that?

GORDON. Gents, you had better go. No use having trouble.

HOLLIS. All right, Joe. When you get over your temper, we will see you.

CARTER *(to Gordon).* I don't like your looks. I think you are a busy body and sort of an old woman.

GORDON. And my opinion of you sir, is that you are a darn scoundrel.

(Carter strikes at Gordon who wards the blow. Gordon knocks him against table and jumps back to beside Bronco who has pistols leveled at Hollis and Carter.)

BRONCO JOE. Down with your shooting irons or I'll kill you both.

CARTER. I'll strike you again.

HOLLIS *(to Carter).* Hush! You have spoiled all the work we have done.

(Both exit and seen to pass widow. Hold position till they pass window.)

BRONCO JOE. Fine customers for a first-class salon. *(Calls.)* Judson. *(Going up.)* Where's that barkeeper?

GORDON *(turns and see Louise.)* My god! Louise! Why are you here?

LOUISE. Hush! I wanted to clear your good name and came here to watch for Carter and Hollis. Also, to seek you. I felt that you would come to Red Rock. Don't look so strangely at me.

GORDON. Do you care for — for this outlaw?

LOUISE. No, Tom. When Frances Veshell came to us as a servant she said her father lived at Fort Hill. Then she received a letter, you know her history, her father being dead. Bronco Joe sends for her, and I take her place. Don't be angry, it was done to help you.

GORDON. Angry, Louise? No. Only vexed. This disguise, the danger, everything that a woman should never see or hear. This is a vile corner of hell in the West. Why did that man pursue you?

LOUISE. He questioned me as to where I came from, if I had ever lived in Kansas City, then he put his arm around my waist and I screamed and ran. I suspect him to be Carter.

(Bronco Joe cautiously down, listens.)

GORDON. I have the same suspicions, but I am not sure. Did you see Alice?

LOUISE. No. I called several times after you left home, but each time was told that show could not be seen.

GORDON. Can she think me guilty?

LOUISE. No, but her father will prevent you from seeing her.

GORDON. I have committed no crime — betrayed. How Carter learned the secret of the gold shipment is a mystery to me. Well, it has changed my whole life and I will not rest until I have forced the truth from him.

BRONCO JOE. *(between them)*. So, you two know each other, eh? Wrong party after the property. Well, you don't get it, got that?

(Stage lights gradually down.)

GORDON. Joe, you have known me a month. Have I ever acted wrong? Send Jordon out and I will explain.

BRONCO JOE *(going to Jorden)*. Jorden, I forgot the hug meat. Go over to the shop and get it. *(Jorden exits.)* Now, you can spell, got that?

GORDON. Bronco, you're a little rough, but any one can bank on you. This is not Louise Voshall, but my sister Louise Gordon. Frances Voshall is her maid and from her she learned all the particulars.

BRONCO JOE *(taking off hat)*. A gal! Well, hang me, if I don't like yer even if yer be. Got that? But what brings her here?

GORDON. A month ago, I was cashier of the Wells-Fargo Express Company at Kansas City and engaged to marry the Supt's daughter. The bookkeeper was also in love with her and determined to break our engagement. He found out by some means that a shipment of gold was to be made —

BRONCO JOE. I got that, go on —

GORDON. —and attempted a plan by which to change the boxes. Duplicate boxes of lead arrived, but the shipment of gold was postponed. The bookkeeper and another clerk who was in league with him could not account for the boxes, and when questioned, accused me of betraying the office secrets and revealed the entire conversation between Mr. Bennett and myself.

BRONCO JOE. How did they learn it?

GORDON. That is a mystery. We were discharged. I thought it possible they might come here, so disguised myself, pretended to be a furs dealer and the rest you know.

BRONCO. I got that. And you Frank, I mean Miss —

LOUISE. Call me Frank. My brother left home and we had no idea where he had gone, but he mentioned Red Rock and Yuma. I tried to see his sweetheart but failed. Then there came a letter from you to Frances Voshell, I persuaded her to let me come in her place. I wanted to locate Carter and Hollis if possible, clear my brother's name and perhaps find him.

BRONCO JOE. And this Hollis and Carter — ?

LOUISE. Are the two men who have just left here.

BRONCO JOE. And they suspected you of being a woman. What are they doing here?

GORDON. I don't know. My sister is positive of their identity, but I am not.

BRONCO JOE. Want to know how they got the secret? Want to know what they are up to now? Got that? Well, I'll find out. You stay around Frank, since your absence would excite their suspicion, and you go on being a furs dealer.

GORDON. If I succeed in establishing my innocence, Joe, I won't forget you.

LOUISE. And a sister's gratitude will ever be yours.

BRONCO JOE. Why Frank what's the use of that? I like you, and that covers the range.

(Enter Judson)

JUDSON. The meat will be over.

BRONCO JOE. Light the lamps. Can you cook, Frank?

LOUISE. You bet I can. Just point out what you want fried, boiled or sizzled.

BRONCO JOE *(to Gordon.)* Did you hear that? Ain't she a corker? Darned if I ain't proud of you. Get that?

GORDON. Can I see Frank for a moment?

BRONCO JOE. Sure, you know the room. No one will disturb you.

GORDON. Thank you, Joe.

(He exits.)

LOUISE. How do you like your stew, Joe, or your meat, rare or well done?

BRONCO JOE. Ha, ha! The way you want it, Kid.

LOUISE. Then I will boil it. Got that?

(She exits.)

BRONCO JOE. There's a boy for you! Now get ready, Jim. I expect a rush tonight.

JUDSON. Crazy Dog is coming tonight, Joe.

BRONCO JOE. Who told you?

JUDSON. He did.

BRONCO JOE. Did he know I was here?

JUDSON. No, guess not.

BRONCO JOE. Well, all right. I'll have to kill him. Got that? We had a picnic last winter and I laid him up. This time I'll put sand on him to keep the rain off. Glad you told me.

JUDSON. I didn't know you knew him.

BRONCO JOE. So Crazy Dog is coming, eh? I thought he would sooner or later. Well, I'll make a good injun out of him. Got that?

(Enter Joshua.)

JOSHUA. Say, be this a tavern?

BRONCO JOE. Christopher Columbus! Where do you hail from?

JOSHUA. I just asked you if this be a tavern.

BRONCO JOE. No sir. It's a high-toned saloon and never shuts. What did you want, stranger?

JOSHUA. Well, I figured it out this way, that if this place was a tavern, I'd stop here, get my feed and sleep for a day or two while I look around. I bought a lot of mining stock up East and run down to look over the mines.

BRONCO JOE. What mines?

JOSHUA. The Silver Angel and The Never End.

BRONCO JOE. Yes, I know them. Did anyone ever sell you a gold brick? Well, your gold mines are the same thing. We can put you up plain sailing, no frills.

JOSHUA. Oh, anything will do me. Have any sport about here, any Indians?

BRONCO JOE. There isn't an injun within forty miles of here.

JOSHUA. Heard a lot about them cusses. I would like to see a couple.

(Enter Solitaire.)

SOLITAIRE. Ah, captain, I salute you, saw you coming up the hills. You remind me very much of General Gush who commanded the 10th Brigade at Pine Bluff. I saved his life at that fight. Notice this? *(Points at badge.)* He was a born fighter, brave as a tiger and you look his image to a tea. Oh, we will never see them good old days again.

JOSHUA. Say, I'll take a wrestler out of you in a minute.

SOLITAIRE. Wrestle? What for, dear sir?

JOSHUA. For trying to make me believe that darn lie.

SOLITAIRE. A lie, sir? Do you know my record?

JOSHUA. You have no record, darn ye. I was at the battle of Pine Bluff and no such general was there.

SOLITAIRE *(extending hand).* Brother!

JOSHUA. Get out. The only thing you ever fought for is whiskey.

SOLITAIRE. Bronco, will you stand by and see me abused by this concentrated farm product of corn, mostly corn? Give me a drink to take the taste out of my mouth. When the boys at the Fort hear this, they will be savage. Only last month a man insulted me and the boys hung him. Yes sir, hung him. Where's the drink, Joe?

BRONCO JOE. Where's the money?

SOLITAIRE. I didn't mean liquor, Joe, just water.

JOSHUA *(at table).* How long were you in the army?

SOLITAIRE. None of your business.

(Solitaire exits.)

JOSHUA *(jumps up).* I calculate I'll have fun around here. Got any more natives like that? Well, do I longer a spell with you, mister?

BRONCO JOE. Cost you four a day. Got that? And in advance.

JOSHUA. Afeared I'd run away, eh? I'm no skin.

BRONCO JOE. See here, yank, did you come in here for a fight or to get vittles and lodging? You can have either. But be quick about it. Got that? Now my price is four dollars. What is it to be?

JOSHUA. Ain't yar kind of steep?

BRONCO JOE. Not when we pay eleven dollars a barrel for flour and fifty cents a pound for butter and seventy-five cents a pound of coffee and —

JOSHUA. Hold em! That will do. Here's eight dollars. Reckon it's cheaper. Now where's the bank?

(Judson enters.)

BRONCO JOE. Show this tenderfoot to the attic over the barn.

JOSHUA. I spose if I had a room on the ground floor it would cost eight dollars a minute. Oh, I'll get acquainted here and like it first rate.

JUDSON. Come on country.

(He exits.)

JOSHUA. I'll take a fall out of him as a starter.

(He exits. Enter Texas Jake.)

TEXAS JAKE. Hello Joe. Tkere's a party over here from Fort Mill and I invited them up.

(Enter three supers and four ladies followed by Solitaire. They take tables left. Enter Judson, behind bar. Enter Gordon and Louise. Gordon leans on bar at back. Louise at door.)

BRONCO JOE. Now for the entertainment. Got that? The first man that pounds on the table with a beer glass or shoots out the light will answer to me. Got that? Rose sing a song.

(Rose specialty. Judson specialty. Fanny specialty. During Fanny's specialty Joshua enters and listens.)

JOSHUA. Dame me, if I can't sling a foot.

(Joshua specialty.)

BRONCO JOE. Say Frank — Gents and laides, this is my boy, Frank, and I want everyone to respect him, got that?

SOLITAIRE *(rising).* As a veteran of three wars and meeting a great many people, I will say that Frank is the best people I ever met. When I stood ay the fall of Richmond —

BRONCO JOE. Gol darn yer sit down!

(Solitaire falls in seat.)

BRONCO JOE. *(who has been whispering to Louise).* My boy Frank will give us "—" (name of song.)

(Louise specialty. During song enter Sergeant Cooney. At end of specialty:)

BRONCO JOE. Gents, Sergeant Cooney.

SOLITAIRE *(rising)*. Salute!

BRONCO JOE. Set down! *(Solitaire falls.)* The sergeant and Jim will oblige. *(During specialty Bronco Joe serves drinks. At end of specialty:)* Come girls!

(Laura specialty. During this turn Carter and Hollis look in window. Judson sees them and mentions to Bronco Joe who peers around bar. Carter retires. Crazy Dog looks in window. At end of specialty, they retire.)

JUDSON *(aside to Bronco)*. I wonder if they are up to anything.

BRONCO JOE. No. Don't like to come in. Clear the tables. All ready for the dance.

SOLITAIRE. This reminds me of a dance I did just before the battle of—

BRONCO JOE. Set down.

COONEY. Respect that man! He is the finest liar the army ever produced.

(Enter Rattlesnake Pete.)

PETE. I'm a bad man from Dead Man's Gulch. *(Leans against bar, drawing revolver.)* I want to see blood. Who wants to lose an ear? Come speak up, or I'll kill one of yar for luck. Ain't had a killing in three days. Whoopee! *(Replaces pistol. Walks around tables snapping fingers in men's faces.)* I'm hungry for fear. *(All shriek away from him. Judson follows him around.)* Here you! Don't follow my trail or I'll drop yar. I'll blow my breath in your face and kill you.

JUDSON. Won't you shake hands, Pete?

PETE. You're too small to waste a cartridge on. You, stranger. Shake.

(Judson takes both hands, supposed to squeeze them in strong grip. Pete begins to squirm, then dance, twist about, jumps up and down, then on knees in pain. Judson lets go and Pete falls. Kicks him. He rises, kicks him off. All laugh. Music for dance.)

BRONCO JOE. Choose your gal! Let her go. *(Music.)* I'll dance with my boy.

(Dances with Louise. During dance Crazy Dog enters. Carter at window. Retires. Crazy Dog cautiously down, watched by Gordon. Crazy Dog makes a lunge at Bronco Joe as he waltzes from left to right with Louise. Arm caught by Gordon.)

GORDON. You villain!

(Music stops. Cowboys reach for guns.)

BRONCO JOE. Stand back everybody! No man must interfere. Got that? This man has tried to kill me before. *(Draws knife.)* Now he must fight right here.

LOUISE. Joe, he may kill you. Don't Joe!

BRONCO JOE. Don't be scared Frank. This is my regular business. Come on you dog.

(All characters draw to one side close to tables leaving stage open. Music by orchestra. Knife fight, when Bronco Joe stabs Crazy Dog. Women all crowd in centre.)

BRONCO JOE. Down on your knees, gals!

(Women on knees centre. Cowboys in front. Solitaire under table. Joshua under table. Supers run behind bar.)

GORDON. Make another step and we fire!

Curtain

End Act Two

Act Three

Drop representing Wichita Mountains. Perspective. High set rock oblique set near drop, painting to match. Wood wings. Set telegraph office right. Window facing front and low enough to show table. Instrument to be heard ticking. Door in wing facing stage. Telegraph bars fastened to wing as if on the roof. Glass insulated wires. Table and chair in office. Railroad tracks cross the stage. Practical switch to throw track. Ground cloth to show ties, stone bedding, grass, and leaves. Working engine and express car to come on from left.

At rise of curtain Sherley discovered in office, ticking of instruments heard. Enter Solitaire and Joshua.

SOLITAIRE. Why I can get anything from this road. Just notice how quick he will send my telegram. Mr. Sherley, this is Mr. Glue who is going to open a couple of gold mines and ship over this road. Shove this message along, Joe, collect. Yes, Mr. Glue, this is the best road in this country. I helped to lay the first rail, see this?

SHERLEY. You've certainly got your nerve with you. I can't send this message.

SOLITAIRE. What ails it?

SHERLEY. You must prepay it. Collect message don't go today.

SOLITAIRE. By jumping Christopher not an ounce of our ore will be sent over this skinflint road.

JOSHUA. What did you send for? *(Reads message.)* "George E. Duback, Assistant. Just opened a couple of gold mines. Banker Joshua Glue, the Massachusetts millionaire man is my guest, desires a special car to Kansas City. We are going to hire five hundred men and a parcel of Chinese in Chicago and bring 'em over your road. Col. Sacage." Well, hang you up for gall. Talk about shipping ore, why darn your picture you don't know where the mines are. *(Tears up telegram.)*

SOLITAIRE. Sir, I know every inch of this soil. I lost 75,000 in one mine alone. The mines you want are about a mile above this gully on the fill. A very fine spot for a mine but damn bad for gold.

JOSHUA. You tarnation bull pup, I'll take a fall out of you in a "minnet." Who the deuce would dig a hole in this wilderness if it wasn't for gold? Here's the chart! Look at that!

SOLITAIRE. Pray, dear sir, what would you have me do? Folks come out here, dig a hold, then go back and sell the stock to develop the mine. All you ever get is the stock certificates.

JOSHUA. Do you mean to say that there is no gold in this mine?

SOLITAIRE. Not a speck, sir, I am an old mining engineer, and have developed more mines in this section than any five men. I was assayer here for two years. Notice this?

JOSHUA. You're a liar!

SOLITAIRE. Oh, of course, take refuse in personalities, brow beat an old expert you know it all, go, find your darn old mine!

(Joshua seizes Solitaire around the waist. They shuffle when Joshua trips Solitaire up and sets on him.)

JOSHUA. By Rueben, I told you I'd do it!

(Punches him.)

SOLITAIRE. Let go of my nose! Ouch! Help! Help! Oh, enough! Enough!

JOSHUA. Yer sich a darn liar I can't believe yer.

SOLITAIRE. I'll have the law. I used to be lawyer.

JOSHUA. Shut up! Open yer potato trap agin and I'll kick yer. *(Rises.)* No gold in my mine, eh? Want it yerself, I reckon. Now get up and point it out.

(Solitaire rises slowly. As he is doing so, Joshua pulls out a flask so that Solitaire comes in contact with it as he rises. Solitaire quick on feet. Takes a drink.)

SOLITAIRE. Very kind, sir. I really don't mind having such exercise. It limbers one up. I used to be a very fine wrestler, in my younger days.

JOSHUA. If you don't stop lying to me, I'll tie my foot in your throat.

SOLITAIRE. Oh! Of course, use your brute strength against intellect. You want to be the hero. I am nobody — never was anybody — you are everything.

JOSHUA. I calculate I'm more than you be. Seen more — know more. I seen a man down there in Vermont lift a horse and toss him over his head.

SOLITAIRE. Yes. How close were you to the man?

JOSHUA. About twenty feet.

SOLITAIRE. And you don't recognize me?

JOSHUA. Recognize yer?

SOLITAIRE. Yes. I'm the man that tossed that horse.

JOSHUA. Well, darn you! *(Kicks Solitaire, who runs off.)* I invented that horse story to see what he would say. Darn cuss claimed to be the man.

Hold on there! Don't yer try and sneak away. I wouldn't be lost in this wilderness fer twenty-five cents.

(He exits. Ener Carter and Hollis.)

CARTER. Well, I hope we won't make a failure of it. Crazy Dog failed to kill Bronco Joe and seize the boy, so we don't really know if the boy is Louise Gordon, disguised or not.

HOLLIS. You are always croaking. You see shadows everywhere. I used to live in this country, as I knew what I am doing. *(Up to window.)* Express stop here?

SHERLEY. No sir.

HOLLIS. I am sorry to hear that. A friend of ours fell from his horse and fractured his leg and we want to get him on the first train to Fort Worth. Do you suppose they'd stop if we send the conductor a telegram?

SHERLEY. I don't think so.

CARTER. Is the train generally on time?

SHERLEY. Not always.

HOLLIS. The train slacks up here anyway?

SHERLEY. No sir.

CARTER. It's a darn outrage. Our friend is suffering and needs medical aid.

SHERLEY. There is another train that reaches here forty minutes after the express. That will stop for you.

HOLLIS *(aside to Carter)*. We have only forty minutes to do the job. The work must be rapid.

CARTER. What time did you say the express would pass?

SHERLEY. Can't tell you, sir. It's due at ten o'clock. It may be on time and it may be one or two hours late.

(Hollis and Carter over to centre.)

HOLLIS. We must get rid of that fellow or tie him up. Now Carter, remember this. That each one of us has a part to do in this hold up and everyone must do his work and do it quick.

CARTER. Then we should see the men and instruct them.

HOLLIS. Yes, and map out a plan to nail this agent. I'm a telegraph operator myself, so we can easily ascertain where the train is located then cut the wires.

(They exit. Enter Bronco Joe and Louise.)

BRONCO JOE. Here is the spot, Frank. Here's where the Marshall stood, got that? I came along here and gave him a lift. It was before the railroad was built. I just wanted to point out the spot to you. If you're tried, set down.

LOUISE. Joe, the money the Marshall left for Frances. Have you put it away for her? She is a quiet girl and no one in the world but herself. This money would help her in many ways.

BRONCO JOE. Frank, I won't lie to you. I spent that money on the saloon but I have put aside a thousand in gold and will give it to you to take home.

LOUISE. How much did the Marshall give you?

BRONCO JOE. Two thousand dollars cash. *(Pause.)* I hate to think of your going back. Kinda takes the life out of me. Never had any one around. *(Sets on back side of Louise. She rises and goes up stage.)* Didn't offend yer, did I?

LOUISE. No, Joe.

BRONCO JOE. I 'spose they miss yer mighty back at home.

LOUISE. Yes, a little.

BRONCO JOE. Folks don't call now?

LOUISE. Yes, just the same.

BRONCO JOE. I 'spose they call to talk about you.

LOUISE. I presume they do, my being absent.

BRONCO JOE. What ails yer, Frank? Afeard I'm going to make love to you, eh?

LOUISE. You wouldn't do that Joe.

BRONCO JOE. Say, Frank, if I loved yer, I'd let my heart bust before I'd tell yer, so don't be afeerd of Joe.

LOUISE. Our lives are so different, Joe. They would never run together. If you were in the city you would pine for the hills and if I remained here, I would pine for the city. So, you see how much better it would be for us to take our right place in the world. I like you Joe and you can like me as Frank, sort of chums like. The sun is going down Joe, let us hurry on. *(Exits.)*

BRONCO JOE. She's right. I'd be a gauk in a big city and shame her. I'm darn glad I didn't tell her I loved her and she's too young to guess at it.

(He exits. Enter Cooney and Solitaire.)

COONEY. I don't care a fig what ye have to do. The fool can find his own way out. What possessed him to go on the mountain?

SOLITAIRE. We own a couple of mines. I have fifty per cent of the gold, so I took him up to look 'em over.

COONEY. Faith and its cut wood ye will do now. You have had rations long enough without working. So, come along wid yer and cut the wood for the mail carriers quarters.

(He exits.)

SOLITAIRE. Cut wood? Well, I haven't cut wood since my escape from Libby Prison and —

(Enter Rose.)

ROSE. Hello Solitaire. Cutting wood?

SOLITAIRE. No indeed. I was just up to my gold mine cutting away the brush. Rose, sit down. I want to say something. I hear that you have saved some money. Now I'm not poor. I have twenty thousand in gold in a bank in Frisco. I own half interest in two gold mines. I save every cent — ask me why?

ROSE. Why?

SOLITAIRE. So, I can give the girl who marries me a great send off. I gave my first wife a diamond necklace worth over five thousand. She died and her relatives claimed the diamonds.

ROSE. So, you are going to marry again?

SOLITAIRE. Yes. I want to build a magnificent mansion in Denver. I have all the plans. Rose will you be the lucky woman?

ROSE. Why of course.

SOLITAIRE. Do you mean it?

ROSE. Sure thing. I'm sort of lonely.

SOLITAIRE *(about to embrace her)*. Come to my heart.

(Enter Cooney, steps between them, takes Solitaire by ear).

COONEY. You cut wood first.

(He leads him off. Rose laughing. Enter Gordon.)

GORDON. If I can overtake Louise, I will — Good evening Rose. Rather late to be so far from Red Rock.

ROSE. Oh no. It's only a couple of miles. I came here to meet a Jack Baker.

GORDON. Baker?

ROSE. Are you surprised? Look here Doc, I have tried to find out if you cared for me or not. You act so strangely. Some days you're awful nice, set and talk with me, then the next day I don't see you and can't find you.

GORDON. So, you are to meet Jack Baker — good evening.

ROSE *(restraining him)*. Doc, do you care? Say the word and I will go with you. You're different from the men about here.

GORDON. Rose, do you want my eternal gratitude?

ROSE. Yes, Doc.

GORDON. Then see this man, Baker. Found out his real name and how he come here. Does he like you?

ROSE. Oh, in his way. Sort of crazy over me. He made me promise to meet him here at sundown. Says he will make me rich.

GORDON. Make you rich? Will you do as I ask?

ROSE. I will try, Doc. But don't be so cold and distant to me. If I learn anything from Baker, where shall I find you?

GORDON. At Bronco Joe's.

(He exits. Enter Hollis, seizing her wrist.)

HOLLIS. So you have a lover, eh?

ROSE. No. Why, I've known Doc ever so long.

HOLLIS. You haint known him over two months.

ROSE. Say, did you ask me to come here to quarrel? Let go of my wrist. What do you think I am?

HOLLIS. Rose, I confess it. I am jealous of you and after tonight I want you to leave here and go with me. Will you?

ROSE. Why, I know nothing about you, Mr. Baker. The man I trust, must trust me. I don't propose to go around the country as a figure head.

HOLLIS. What do you want to know?

ROSE. Everything. Your name may be Baker or it may be Smith or Jones. You can be a tenderfoot afraid of his shadow or you may have nerve.

HOLLIS. Oh, I see. You want to know what kind of a man I am. Well, I'm a road agent.

ROSE. Get out!

HOLLIS. I am going to hold up the express tonight. It carries fifty thousand.

ROSE. How do you know?

HOLLIS. I know, that's enough.

ROSE. Yes, for you but not for me. Now tell me all about it.

HOLLIS. I swear to you it is right. Two months ago, I was a clerk in the office of the Wells-Fargo Express. My partner was also there. He loved the superintendent's daughter and to find out if it was true that she loved the cashier I fixed wires to the telephone and placing a receiver in my hat overheard the conversation. She was in love with the cashier, and he was to go over the road taking fifty thousand. Carter, the clerk, determined upon revenge. The shipment was delayed, and we were accused. Carter turned on the cashier and told the superintendent that Gordon had betrayed the secret.

ROSE. And this Gordon loved the superintendent's daughter?

HOLLIS. What ails you?

ROSE. My head aches. Tell me all.

HOLLIS. Well, Carter and I skipped out and came here. We knew the money would come sooner or later, so we planted a messenger. Yesterday he wired us. The money will be here tonight.

ROSE. Your name is not Baker?

HOLLIS. No. You can call me Hollis. I have told you all Rose. Will you join me tonight? We are sure to secure the money and I will stick by you through thick and thin.

ROSE. What was the name of the cashier?

HOLLIS. Tom Gordon. Do you know, I suspected Doc Holliday of being Gordon until you told me you had known him.

ROSE. Why he's a fare dealer. Never been East. Came from Frisco.

HOLLIS. Do you care for him?

ROSE. Now what put that into your head?

HOLLIS. Because I love you Rose. Promise me you will be here tonight.

ROSE. All right. Do I get a whack at that money?

HOLLIS. Rose, you shall have half of my share.

ROSE *(going left)*. I'll be here. I kind of like you now since you have told me all about yourself.

HOLLIS. And when you come to know me better you will love me.

(Both exit. Enter Joshua.)

JOSHUA. I'll bet my hide, I'm lost. I figured out on a rock the way I came. Now I can't find the damn rock. *(Looks overhead.)* That darn tramp sneaked off and left me. Hello, here's the station, so I ain't lost and there came that bum barkeeper. I wonder what he's up to.

(He retires back of rock, listens. Enter Carter and Judson.)

CARTER. Do you mean to say that Bronco Joe would refuse to take a hand in the hold up?

JUDSON. Say — *(Looks around.)* Bronco makes believe he is a hard to people what don't know any different, just to find out what they are up to.

CARTER. What for?

JUDSON. Why he's a deputy U. S Marshall. He waits until the trick is done, then he leads his man and goes for the reward. We must get out of this country quick. Where is Hollis? Say, he's stuck on Rose, ain't he? I hope he won't let her in on this job.

CARTER. Oh, he's too smart for that. He should be here now. We will walk down the gully and meet him.

(Both exit. Enter Joshua.)

JOSHUA. By ginger, this is a lovely country. Going to have a hold up. Reckon it's a sort of dance. Well, I'll shake a foot with them. Can't be stuck up. *(Looks off left.)* Hang me up to freeze, if here don't come.

(He runs back of rock. Enter Cooney with axe.)

COONEY. Come on Solitaire. It's a fine appetite ye'll be having this night. *(Enter Solitaire loaded down with wood, all sizes, parts of trees.)* It's glad ye ought to be for the chance. When Maggie Murphy comes and we open a place or buy out Bronco Joe I'll let ye cut wood for me ever day. Come on.

(He exits.)

SOLITAIRE. I'd sooner be an Indian. I remember once when I was an Indian, I had nothing to do but eat. Oh, why did I ever turn pale face to cut wood?

(During the above, Joshua slips out, places foot in front of Solitaire and as Solitaire moves, he falls over foot. Wood to fall off shoulder up stage. Supposed to strike Solitaire.)

JOSHUA. Consarn yer hide, can't yer see where yer be going? *(Holding foot in hand.)*

SOLITAIRE *(sitting up)*. When I commanded the plantation builders on the Rap-er-hanick I cut down over five acre of timber. Notice this?

JOSHUA. Get up darn yer! Say, what's a hold up?

SOLITAIRE. Hold up? In the language of the frontier, it means to rob, to violently abstract money from the owner and use it fer yourself. When I was president of the Indian college, I used to translate Cherokee. Notice this?

JOSHUA. Well, there's going to be a hold up here tonight and I want to see it.

SOLITAIRE. Do you know what it means to be caught? We might — *(heads close together)* — be witnesses and point out the parties for part of the reward. If the train is held up there is sure to be a reward. Some years ago, I held up a train when I was provost marshal and caught over five robbers red handed. Sh!

(They retire left. Enter Hollis and Carter carrying cowboy between them. Hollis by Judson and two centre who stand watching.)

HOLLIS. Here is our friend, Mr. Agent. Can he set in there?

SHERLEY. Yes.

(He turns to open door when cowboy from right goes to Sherley and levels gun at Sherley. As Sherley opens door they pass in Hollis, seizes Sherley, drawing his arms back. Carter holds revolver at his head. The cowboy ties Sherley to chair and gags him. While this is being done enter Solitaire and Joshua who come down cautiously to see what is the matter when cowboys at window see them.)

SOLITAIRE *(looking in door)*. Jumping Christopher!

(He runs off, cowboy throws rope after him. Solitaire places it about his body. Hollis and Carter from house. Stage darkens. Joshua runs off. Cowboy throws rope. Same business, then cowboys pull them to stage.)

SOLITAIRE. What is the meaning of this outrage? Do you know who I am? This indignity will arouse the regular army to frenzy. Notice this?

JOSHUA. Darn you. But you'll pay for this. Let me leave and I'll wrestle every darnation one of yer.

CARTER. Gag those fools and throw them in the brush. We have no time to waste.

(They bind and gag Joshua and Solitaire.)

HOLLIS. Throw that yank behind the rocks. Let the snakes have fun with him.

(Cowboys retire with Joshua and return.)

CARTER. Now dump the regular army into the brush.

HOLLIS. I'll see how much time we have.

(He enters station, begins telegraphing.)

CARTER. Well, what time?

HOLLIS. Not over four minutes. She's on time. Cut the wires Judson.

(Hollis up to truck with red lamp. Places it centre, then turns switch. Judson runs off left.)

CARTER. Judson and I will look after the express car. Cover the engineer and fire while Denver Dick stations the Indians.

(Whistle in distance.)

HOLLIS. She's coming. To your places!

(All place handkerchief over faces and exit. Carter and Judson retire. Sharp whistle. Engine effect. Turn on steam. Engine slowly to red light.)

ENGINEER. What is that signal for?

HOLLIS. For you. Throw up hands and get down and be quick.

(Marchs them off. Enter Carter and Judson.)

CARTER. Open this car or we will blow it open. *(Hammers on car.)* Open! Open this car or we'll blew it open! Quick Judson, the dynamite.

(They crowd about car, then run off right. At the moment they leave the stage, explosion. Car door and side of car fall out showing interior of car with messenger on his back. Carter on quick, jumps in car. Judson with gun on guard. Carter feels pockets of messenger, secures keys, opens safe.)

CARTER. The money is here but not in gold.

(He jumps out of car. Three shots heard off left. Enter Hollis, Cowboys and supers bringing on Bennett bound and handkerchief over mouth. Enter Alice and Tip.)

CARTER. We want no prisoners!

HOLLIS. Look again and tell me if you will not hold these people?

CARTER *(aside)*. Alice! *(Aloud.)* Boys take this lady into camp. You know where. And take this man and girl over on Bitter Rock Mountain and lose them in the brush.

JOSHUA *(runs on)*. Here come the soldiers! Gosh hang it, we have yer now.

CARTER. You will never get us alive!

(He fires at Joshua who falls to avoid the shot and Carter exits.)

HOLLIS. Quick!

(Cowboys run off leaving rest of characters. Enter Rose, Gordon, Bronco Joe, Louise and Cooney. They rush on. Gordon down to Bennett. They unbind them.)

COONEY Maggie dearest, if yer dead tell me so for me hearty's bumping with fear.

GORDON. Mr. Bennett, we are in time.

BENNETT. Who are you sir?

GORDON. Tom Gordon who tricked these villains.

BRONCO JOE. So you're Mr. Bennett. Here Rose, come here. To this girl we owe all information. And Mr. Gordon is an innocent man, and his sister Louise a gal to be proud of.

BENNETT *(to Rose)*. I will certainly find a suitable reward.

ROSE. Won't want a reward sir. Hollis told me he found out about the money by fixing up a telephone in your office, then saying that Mr. Gordon told them.

BENNETT. Gordon your hand. Alice? Where is Alice?

GORDON. Was she with you?

BENNETT. My God, they have taken her away.

GORDON. Mr. Glue, you stand ground here. We will pursue the villains.

(He runs off.)

BRONCO JOE. I am with you. *(To Louise.)* If I don't return every thing I own is yours.

LOUISE. I will go with you.

BRONCO JOE. No! No! Mr. Bennett she must not go. *(Forces her in Bennett's arms.)* Hold her safe in your arms. Good-bye Frank.

LOUISE. Let me go! Let me go!

BENNETT. Hush, Louise.

COONEY. I'm off to the garrison. *(Exits.)*

JOSHUA *(rising)*. Safe at last. And I've seen a hold up.

(Solitaire rolls on, gag off, arms bound, rolls to centre.)

SOLITAIRE *(sitting up)*. Hurry for the Union. The good old days of war have come again. Listen! Hear the shots? Untie me Joshua and lead me into the fight.

(Joshua unties him.)

JOSHUA. Why don't you go.

SOLITAIRE. And leave these ladies to the mercy of the Indians? Never!

(Shot fired from over rock. Bennet staggers, falls centre. Solitaire runs off. Joshua off. Louise raises gun. Head seen over rock. She fires, he falls.)

ROSE *(Raises Bennett's head)*. Are you hurt much? Sir? What shall we do?

LOUISE. Don't be afraid. I'll stand guard till I drop.

(Solitaire peeps on. Joshua same position peeps on. Tip still sitting on stage against rock. Enter Cooney and six Solders. As he enters Louise staggers, is caught by Cooney. Soldiers crowd around Rose and Bennett. Soldier unties Tip. Both rise and shake hands. Picture.)

Curtain

End of Act Three

Act Four

Scene 1

Red River Canyon. Morning.

Enter Solitaire and Joshua, each with gun.

SOLITAIRE. Ah! This seems like the good old days when the stirring scenes of carnage, the thrilling episodes, marvelous escapes, made me strong. And the shriek of the shell, the boom of the canon, the clash of the sabre and the yell of the victorious gave me youth and courage to cut down the enemy!

JOSHUA. Gosh darn it, let's get at 'em.

SOLITAIRE. Steady comrade, I have been through it all and waded knee deep in gore, but never get excited.

JOSHUA. Some of the boys may have been hurt.

SOLITAIRE. Indian warfare is different from our legitimate fighting. Do you remember my commands to be given on the field of battle? Attention! Behind tree! *(Joshua behind imaginary tree.)* Fall flat! *(Joshua falls flat.)* Grass sheet! *(Joshua places gun on toes of shoes.)* Rock picking! *(Joshua turns over on stomach. Gun pointed.)* On feet! *(Joshua rises.)* Now keep your eye open and cover my rear column. Forward! *(Lock step.)* If the enemy coverages, throw on your full center. If they deplore, push out your right wing. If they form a square catch 'em at right ankles or by the leg.

JOSHUA. Supposing they don't do this.

SOLITAIRE. Then run like hell!

(Both exit. Enter Bronco Joe, head bound up. Coat in rags. Limp on from right.)

BRONCO JOE. I'll reach camp — reach Frank — send food — water to the boys — ammunition and soldiers — send —

(He falls over on back, up stage. Enter Tip and Louise. Tip with four pistols in belt, sword, two knives, and gun in hand.)

TIP. Come on. Who's afraid?

LOUISE. Hurry on, Tip. I must find my brother — *(sees Joe.)* Joe! Joe! He can't be dead. Joe! Oh, if he would only look at me.

BRONCO JOE. Is that you boy? Cloudy isn't it? I can't see plain. Help me up Frank.

TIP. I can carry you, Mister.

(They assist Bronco Joe to feet.)

BRONCO JOE. Frank give me your hand I shall feel stronger.

LOUISE *(hands flask)*. Drink Joe. It will do you good. I brought it along in case any one needed it. Have you seen my brother?

BRONCO JOE. He is safe.

LOUISE. I am so thankful for that. Are you hurt much Joe?

BRONCO JOE. The liquor has pulled me straight together. Who is this man?

LOUISE. He is one of the porters from the train. He worked for Mr. Bennett.

BRONCO JOE. Go back to the camp arouse everybody and bring food and ammunition. Take the left trail to Mulberry Creek. They will understand. Got that? Quick man? Don't forget left trail to Mulberry Creek.

TIP. I'm off like a rocket.

BRONCO JOE. Frank, we chased that mob into the canyon, and I started back for food and ammunition. The night was dark, and I tripped and away I went down, down till I landed in the gully. Then knew no more until the warm sun was shinning in my face. I was weak but pulled myself along until I reached here. I am so glad to see you, boy. How is Mr. Bennett?

LOUISE. He is resting quietly. I took the liberty of giving him your room.

BRONCO JOE. Liberty? Why boy, it is all yours. I feel that my time has come Frank and there's no use crowding secrets into the grave, get that? The only human being I ever loved was my mother, until I met you. I love you boy and to a man like me, that means life, soul, all! When I am gone, just bury me. Should I live, forget that I ever told you.

LOUISE. Let us go — go on as quickly as we can. You must have the surgeon.

BRONCO JOE. No use. That fall twisted me up, Frank.

LOUISE. Call me Louise, Joe.

BRONCO JOE. Louise? How tender that does sound when I speak it out aloud. I never called you Louise, only in my dreams and in a whisper when asking my heart to love yer.

LOUISE. Come Joe. Lean on me.

BRONCO JOE. Yes, we will go. Let me have your hand. I'm strong now, Louise. Dear Louise.

(They exit. Lights down.)

Act Four

Scene 2

Lights up in dug out, showing roof made of logs and straw. Rock wings. Mountain drop seen over top of dug out.

Discovered Alice on box, Carter at table.

CARTER. Alice, what I have done was for desperation born of despair, and you are the cause of it. I care nothing for life. Here we are pen'd in and may be killed at any moment. Alice you can redeem my life. I will restore every dollar of the money to your father and live an upright life. I could do so much in this world with your love and encouragement. Alice, have you no word for me?

ALICE. There is no use in repeating my answer. You know it. When I first met you, I like you but when your actions and manners convinced me that you were a man to be unreasonable jealousy and of an overbearing nature, I felt that you only needed an incentive to become thoroughly wicked and an outlaw. That impression has been verified.

CARTER. Well, since this is your opinion, I won't disappoint you. Heaven help you now for you shall never see Tom Gordon again.

ALICE. So, you have contemplated murder as the pinnacle of your wickedness.

CARTER. Not yet. It will be the end of course. But in the meantime, I am going to marry you Indian fashion. The chief will perform the ceremony.

ALICE. You would not dare to do it.

CARTER. Dare? With fifty thousand dollars? Dare? In these mountains one could be a king with that amount of money. Dare? Well, we shall see.

(Enter Gordon attired as an Indian Chief. Comes to centre, folds arms.)

CARTER. Well, who are you?

GORDON. Crazy Dog.

CARTER. Are we well guarded against attack?

GORDON. Indian on guard.

CARTER. You are the chief?

GORDON. Want money.

CARTER. You were paid last night.

GORDON. Want more. *(Points to Alice.)* Pay for squaw.

CARTER. Yes. We are going to be married the moment we are free to escape. You watch her. If she gets away no money. Understand? Guide us out safely and you get one hundred dollars.

GORDON. Pretty squaw. Captain give more.

CARTER. Why you miserable thief, do you mean to force me to pay a ransom now that you have us cooped up in this mountain. You bargained to guide us out of the mountain into New Mexico and I paid you.

GORDON. More risk.

CARTER. What do you want?

GORDON. Blankets for braves and five hundred.

CARTER. Well, I'll even a new deal with you, Chief. The moment we reach the river I will give you five hundred dollars. Here is two hundred. Now I'll find a way clear for me and pretty bride. Bride! Ha! Ha! Bye-bye sweet Alice. Chief, if I am shot and killed, you make that woman your wife.

(He exits ledge.)

ALICE. Infamous scoundrel! *(Looks at Gordon.)* There is no use of appealing to you. Yes. Listen. This man offers you five hundred dollars. I will give you five thousand for liberty and safe return.

GORDON *(looking around).* Alice.

ALICE. Tom!

GORDON. Hush! I am here to save or to die with you. I sent a messenger for troops last night and if it succeeded in reaching Fort Still they are now on their way. During the fight last evening I found a dead Indian, appropriated his dress, thinking I might force my way to you.

ALICE. Where is father?

GORDON. He is safe at Red Rock. Bronco Joe will care for him. He is the messenger I sent for the troops.

ALICE. Can't we escape now, Tom? There is no one here.

GORDON. This dug out is guarded by outlaws. We must depend upon the soldiers. My plan is this — that during the fight, and these outlaws will fight desperately, I will try to carry you away. Carter, believing me to be an Indian will not object.

ALICE. Oh, if we were only at home. I have suffered so much, Tom. So much in thought, that father should believe you guilty.

GORDON. He has had proofs of my innocence, Alice.

(Enter Hollis and Carter.)

HOLLIS. That makes no difference. We will divide now.

CARTER. This chief demands five hundred to guard Alice.

HOLLIS. That is no affair of mine. You want her, I don't. You have forty-eight thousand dollars, give me half. No time like the present.

CARTER. We will divide in Mexico.

HOLLIS. We divide here. Suppose you are shot and I escape. You will be searched, the money recovered while I am penniless in a strange country. No. The division is now.

CARTER. Well so be it. I know your weakness for gambling. Not another cent will I give up. *(Counts money.)* There now, we are square.

(Enter Judson.)

JUDSON. Say, there are Indians moving in the brush. All hands to the front.

(Judson rushes out followed by Hollis.)

CARTER. Come chief.

GORDON. I watch squaw.

CARTER. No you won't. Here. *(Picks up rope, ties her to side of dug out.)* Now you can come back later, but not without me. If I find you with this lady alone during our escape I will kill you.

GORDON. Want me to save her, eh?

CARTER. Yes, but with me by your side. I don't trust you out of my sight. Come.

(When Carter turns, Gordon seizes him by neck and pulls him back over his knees.)

GORDON. Lok at me you villain. I am the man you wronged. Struggle as you will my grip is of iron.

(Judson peeps on ledge — retires.)

ALICE. Tom! Tom, don't have his life on your soul.

GORDON. Better that than your dishonor. *(Throws Carter back, head falls lifeless.)* You scoundrel! *(Jumps up, releases Alice. While this action is going on sabre blade seen coming through door under the bar, raising it.)* He has the money and I will recover it.

(He searches Carter.)

ALICE. Let it go, Tom. If they find you have taken it, they will kill you.

GORDON. At last! *(Rises conceals money.)* Alice we must make an attempt to escape. They will not suspect me in this disguise.

(Bar on door falls, second bar being raised.)

ALICE. Look! Look at the door!

(Enter Hollis and Judson guns pointed.)

HOLLIS. Up with your hands or we fire.

(Alice and Gordon stand left, Alice clinging to Gordon. Door falls in showing Cooney, Tip, Solitaire, Joshua, guns pointed at Hollis and Judson. Hollis and Judson turn and face Cooney. Picture.)

Quick Curtain

Act Four

Scene 3

The Broken Boulder Trail.

Drop representing a cascade in distance. Mountain effect. On left of cascade a huge boulder broken as if split by lightning. Sunlight on cascade.

Enter Cooney.

COONEY. Where the devil are the men? I must have re-in-forcers. Oh, a devil of a time I've had. At the first shot the laggards deserted me. I heard Solitaire say, "Great shoot," and away they went.

(He looks off right. Enter Maggie with a basket.)

MAGGIE. Oh, sir.

COONEY. Maggie Murphy! You're an angel out of a clear sky.

MAGGIE. Sure it's walking I've been and not in a balloon. I heard Tip tell the sergeant at the camp to get ammunition and something to eat for the men, so I got ye some cakes.

COONEY. Cake? Sure, and I can't fight on cake.

MAGGIE. Don't interrupt me. As I was saying I got ye some cake, a jug of fire water, corn beef, mule sausage, pickles and cornstarch. Corn starch is fine for the backbone.

COONEY *(leans gun on wing)*. Begorra and I'll feed it to Tip and Solitaire. The villains left me just at the moment when we had Miss Alice saved. Open the basket darling. I'm starving for drink and food.

MAGGIE. I hurried as quick as my two feet would let me. But the basket was heavy. I brought ye a bottle of spring water.

COONEY *(on bank)*. Come set down.

(Maggie to bank, takes out chunk of bread, leaves basket centre back.)

MAGGIE. Here is a corn beef sandwich.

COONEY *(eating, arm around Maggie)*. This is the first enjoyment of the service. Oh, darling. Only two months and I'll be free.

MAGGIE. Till ye buy out Bronco Joe? And change the place to a store. Joe wants to sell. He was hurted.

COONEY. Hurted?

MAGGIE. Last night he tried, like a brave man he is, to cross the mountains but lost his footing and fall into the gully. Miss Louise found him and now she is nursing him. The surgeon says he busted up his ribs but will be out soon. I'm thinking that Louise has the same complaint I have.

COONEY. What's that?

MAGGIE. Can't you guess it?

COONEY. Oh, it's stupid. I am with hunger. Guess it for me.

MAGGIE. It's in love she is.

COONEY. And so are you. Sure, I knew that. *(Arm around her neck.)* Oh, darling, it's happy we'll be in our snug little home.

(Enter bear over to basket, takes out bottle. Drinks. Then eats apple, cake, bread. While bear is eating Cooney is rocking Maggie in his arms and eating sandwich.)

COONEY. My darling, we will live in the this paradise, wid the flowers and honeysuckles and birds of paradise. Ye can roam over the hills free as a bird.

(Bear gets gun and walks down centre facing Cooney.)

MAGGIE. But the snakes and wild things in the woods.

COONEY. I'm the only wild thing ye will see. Sure and we are free from all reptiles and — *(Sees Bear.)* Holy St. Dennis! Look at that! And he has me gun. *(Grabs Maggie's arm quick.)* Shoo, ye devil, shoo! Shoo! Get out!

(He places Maggie behind him and backs off. Enter Carr, wrestles with bear and exit. Enter Solitaire and Joshua, Solitaire in undershirt and pants, Joshua in red flannel shirt, vest, no coat, pants, no hats.)

SOLITAIRE. Let us invite the aid of the Great Ge-hovia! Pour out torrents on the heads of our enemies. Let them parish in a flood of a mountain torrent. I once cursed a band of Arabs when I was in Egypt and every mother's son of them took sick and died. I found out afterwards, I had been hasty. I cursed the wrong band, but there is no mistake here.

JOSHUA. By ginger, I don't want to see any more Injuns. Tip's gone. I saw Cooney give him a blanket. They tore the clothes off his back to see if he was white. I am tarnation glad to have my life. Why didn't the government chain 'em up? Darn sich a government.

SOLITAIRE. You owe your life to me. Those Injuns knew me by reputation and dare not kill us. Why sir, my death would have aroused the entire army of the frontier. So they take our clothes, then pretend it was a joke on old Solitaire the Indian fighter.

JOSHUA. If I wasn't so darn weak I'd kick you. Why they just played foot ball with you and the yells you made would scare a wild cat.

SOLITAIRE. Yell? of course I have the chalk-taw! Yell? Had I not given that yell we would be dead now at the bottom of some gully. Didn't you see 'em shake? They knew by the yell that I had been a medicine man and was calling for the lightning to flash. Oh, I know my Indian business; why, I was a regular Indian for over four years.

JOSHUA *(tries to kick him but is too weak)*. No use.

SOLITAIRE. What will we do?

(Joshua sees basket, opens it, finds jug, drinks.)

JOSHUA. Here.

SOLITAIRE. Oh! That puts life in me. Saved my life once in South Africa.

JOSHUA. And I feel, gosh darn it, like going back and getting square and I'm going.

SOLITAIRE. It would be murder, sir. Why sir, when I was on an ice flow near the North Pole, one man went back to get change for a dollar so he could settle with an Es-co-maw and he was killed.

JOSHUA *(kicks Solitaire).* Darn you for a liar.

SOLITAIRE. Oh yes, that's right. Be a ruffian.

JOSHUA. Let's have a drink.

SOLITAIRE. No use leaving it here. We can take it with us on the inside. *(Holding jug.)* That's the first joke I ever made West of Sweden. *(Drinks.)*

JOSHUA. Of course you were in Sweden.

(He takes jug, drinks.)

SOLITAIRE. Don't insult me sir. I don't mind being kicked but don't insult me. Don't set on fire the temper of an Ajax.

JOSHUA *(nose in Solitaire's face).* Did you say I insulted you?

SOLITAIRE. No, you did not. I would not permit it, sir. No sir.

(Both exit. Enter Bronco Joe followed by Louise and Bennett.)

BRONCO JOE. I'm all right, boy. Mr. Bennett's daughter and your brother are in the hands of outlaws. No doubt of this since he has not been seen. When your daughter, sir, was last seen by Cooney she was in the dugout in care of an Indian.

BENNETT. Let us move on with all possible haste.

BRONCO JOE *(to soldiers).* Captain, the men are in an old dug out. Take no prisoners. Shoot to kill.

(Exit soldiers.)

BENNETT. Sir, you are a noble fellow and I will not forget you. I am not afraid to face these villains nor have I forgotten how to use a gun. Louise, you had better return to the house.

BRONCO JOE. That's what I have been telling her, sir.

LOUISE. No. You are still weak, Joe and I am going to stand by you. Don't forget that a bullet from his gun will kill as surely as yours.

BENNETT. I will follow the soldiers. Persuade Louise to return.

(He exits.)

BRONCO JOE. Say, boy, if anything happens to you, I'd never forgive myself.

LOUISE. Same with me.

BRONCO JOE. But you might be killed.

LOUISE. Same with you.

BRONCO JOE. But I wouldn't need you if I was dead.

LOUISE. Same with me.

BRONCO JOE. For your brother's sake, go back. *(Shakes her head.)* For my sake, your mother's Will yer make me a coward? Can't ye understand Louise? Louise, don't make me less the man. My duty is there. You have a mother, father, brother — I have nothing. If I fall, no one will sigh, no one will regret and the world will not miss me.

LOUISE. Joe, this is not the hour for sentiment. I love the very danger. The excitement and — *(pause, Joe hangs head)* — I love you!

BRONCO JOE. Thank god! You have made me strong, Boy — Boy — *(Embraces her.)*

LOUISE. You know now why I wish to be near you.

BRONCO JOE. Let me look at that gun. Good! We shall go together. *(Shot heard.)* Listen. *(Shot.)* They are at it. Come boy! We are needed. Shoot to kill!

(They run off. Solitaire and Joshua enter with guns.)

SOLITAIRE. They are at it. We will hide behind a rock and pick off the enemy. I used to pick off the enemy in '62.

JOSHUA. Look! What is that?

SOLITAIRE. Injun.

(He fires.)

JOSHUA. Gosh, if you didn't hit him!

SOLITAIRE. Hit him? I have never failed. The only time I ever missed was when I fired a cannon at the Turks in the Red Sea.

JOSHUA. Look out!

SOLITAIRE. Sneak around this way and when I give the command fire or retreat.

(They hid behind wing. Enter Tip limping.)

TIP. Who fired at me? I was hiding in de bush when some one fires at me.

JOSHUA. Say, you darn fool, yer shot Tip.

SOLITAIRE. Retreat.

(Both exit. Shots heard.)

TIP. Oh, Lord if yer very wanted a chance to help a fool, yer got it now. I don't know which way to go.

(He limps off.)

Curtain

Act Four

Scene 4

The dug out, Red River Canon. Same as Scene 1 only dug out revered.

Carter and Hollis standing on rock right.

CARTER. What do you see?

HOLLIS. The soldiers and Bronco Joe.

CARTER *(glasses to Hollis)*. Look! Don't you recognize Bennett?

HOLLIS. They are at least a mile away. We must leave here and at once.

CARTER. There is only one way out and they cover it.

HOLLIS. We can at least leave here.

CARTER. In that direction we will meet the Apaches. To try and hide in the canon would be folly. The dug out is our only retreat. We must fight.

(Enter Judson.)

JUDSON. Say, see anything yet? I'm tired being shut up in here. Let's go home.

CARTER. Has that Indian moved?

JUDSON. They girl is abusing me. I can't stand it.

HOLLIS *(to centre with Carter)*. I will not remain here to be starved out. The boys can fire a few shots when they come up, then separate. I shall make for the Pecos. You wish to remain because you can't take the girl.

CARTER. Let me think.

HOLLIS. Let her stay. Save yourself man

CARTER. No. I'll kill her first.

HOLLIS. We have no time to argue. Will you go? Yes or no?

CARTER. Yes, and take the girl with me. Open the door, Judson.

(Judson opens door. They all enter. Soldiers enter left on run. Cowboys fire from right over rock. Enter Hollis and Gordon from hut. Enter Carter and Alice from hut.)

HOLLIS. For your lives put distance behind us.

CARTER. Too late! Back! Back!

(Gordon breaks away. Strikes Carter who staggers back. Gordon seizes Alice. Soldiers pour in a fire from guns. Hollis and Carter into dug out. Gordon carries Alice. She faints. Shots heard coming from dug out. Enter Solitaire and Joshua. Tip peeps on left and fires. Cowboy falls back. The door falls and part of roof and side. Judson seen dead. Bronco Joe, Louise and Bennett on.)

BRONCO JOE. Give up if yer want to live.

(Enter Hollis and Carter in shirt sleeves, hands up.)

ALICE *(embraces)*. Father!

GORDON *(drawing off blanket and hat of feathers)*. Mr. Bennett, I demand that these men by placed in the keeping of the Marshall Bronco Joe. I have recovered nearly half of the money and the remainder will be found on Hollis.

HOLLIS. So, you are a Marshall, eh? You traitor!

BRONCO JOE. Bind the prisoners.

SOLITAIRE. I'm one of the best binders in the army.

(Solitaire, Joshua and Tip bind Carter and Hollis.)

BENNETT. Tom, after such dangers I place her hand in yours.

BRONCO JOE. Mr. Gordon, can't yer do the same for us?

(Enter Cooney and Maggie.)

COONEY. Bygorra we're late for the fighting but not fer the giving and taking.

GORDON. Yes, Joe. Louise has told me the story. And after all, the Great Train Robbery has brought happiness to us at least.

(Carter staggers and falls.)

SOLITAIRE. He was shot — and — I shot him!

JOSHUA. Darn me if he ain't dead.

(Picture.)

Curtain

END

www.ingramcontent.com/pod-product-compliance
Ingram Content Group UK Ltd.
Pitfield, Milton Keynes, MK11 3LW, UK
UKHW022010190726
13853UKWH00004B/1844